For my children, Ava, Nolan, and Ronan, who sometimes clean their rooms, and for my dear friend Lauren, without whom this book would not exist.

At daybreak this morning,
you rose with the sun
Leapt out of your bed
and got ready for fun

You played rodeo cowboys and pirates at sea
You stacked up your blocks, and you hosted a tea

Then you strapped on your skates
and mounted your horse
For a One-Person Hula Hoop
Obstacle Course

You built a great train with a long line of chairs

Then drove through the house with your favorite stuffed bears

You played bike riding, art making, dress up, and ball

And raced all your cars through a track down the hall

I'm sure you cleaned up after all that todo

But the mess-making do-no-good bandit came through

He toppled the blocks, made a mess of the playdough

and flipped the toy cars like a giant tornado

He dumped out the toy box and emptied the drawers

Roughed up the dolls and the green dinosaurs

Then he slipped out the door with maniacal laughter

And left us alone in the great toy disaster

Now it's getting late and it may not sound fun

But this room must be cleaned and this mess be undone

So let's make a game and we'll race till we're through

The very first step is to pick up the blue

Find all the blue stuff from teal to cyan

And put it all up just as fast as you can

The navy blue truck and the blue bouncing ball

We picked up a bunch, but can you find them all?

The royal blue book and the jeans by the door

Keep going, keep going, I still see some more

When finally you can't spot a speck that is blue

Race back to me and we'll go to round two

Now that the blue stuff is out of our hair

Let's take a look at the things that you wear

Put clothes in the drawers if you'll wear them again

And put all the rest in the dirty clothes bin

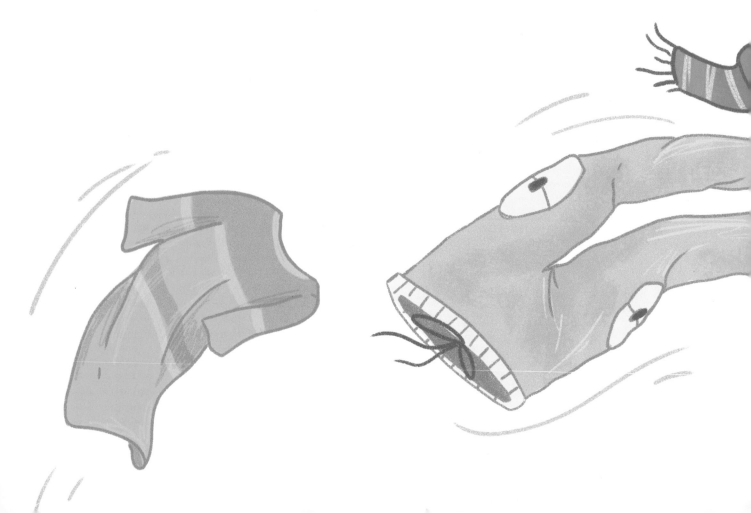

That old smelly sock is just prime for the picking

Quick, snatch it up, the timer is ticking

Get the hat and the pants and don't miss that shoe

We'll turn the next page just as soon as you're through

Let's scan around for the things that make noise

The beep-bopping, ding-making, musical toys

The drum that you bang and your plastic kazoo

The car with the horn and the talking toys too

Pick them up, pick them up, pick them up fast

Let's see which one of us finds something last!

Now for a challenge and you'll do fantastic

This is a test that's a bit more scholastic

Search all around through what's left of the mess

And pick up the things that start with an 'S'

The sailboat, the slinky, the sword and the snake

The squirt gun and sand pail and Superman cape

Keep going until all the 'S' things are gone

Then come back to me when it's time to move on

Now for some counting — I know you can do it.

I'll count out loud and you can get to it

Let's count all the things until you pick up ten

Get ready, get set, here we go, let's begin...

One

Two

Three

Four

Five.....

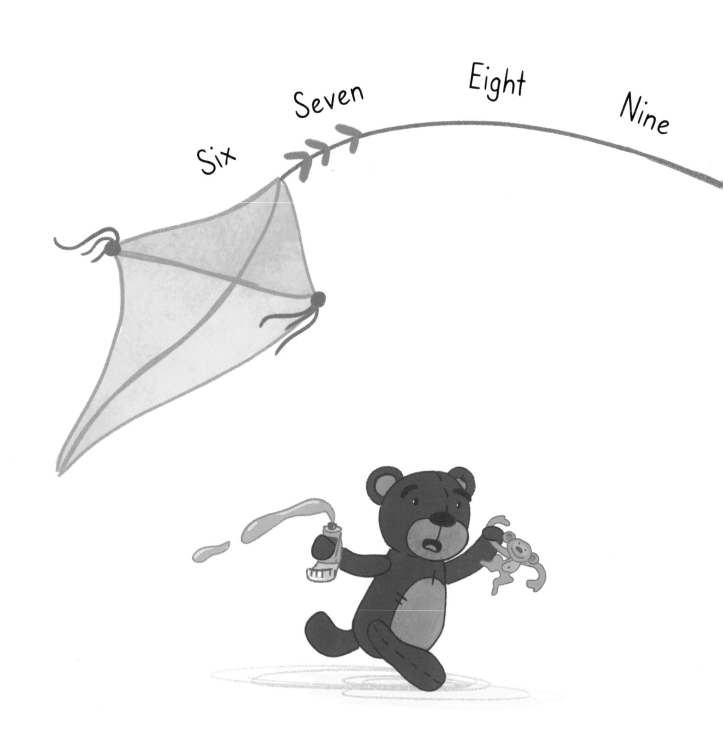

Six   Seven   Eight   Nine

Keep Going!

TEN!

Quick, gather up all the toys that are cuddly

Your floppy pink bunny so warm and so snuggly

Look under the bed, in each crevice and crack

For the toys full of stuffing with seams in the back

Find the soft and the squishy, the toys that are furry

And put them all back where they go in a hurry

Then pick up your teddy from there on the rug

And put him to bed with a kiss and a hug

Let's flip up this game, now you take the lead

Take a look at what's left and decide what we need

Is there one color still scattered around?

Or too many square things,

or too many round?

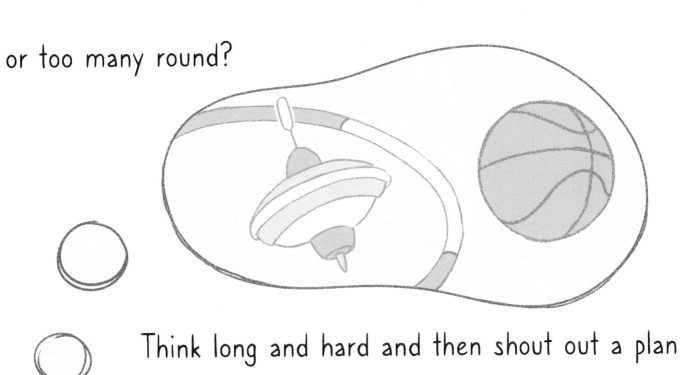

Think long and hard and then shout out a plan

and we'll do it together as fast as we can!

We're at the home stretch now, there's not much to do

We picked up the 'S' things, the clothes, and the blue

Let's set a timer to clean up the rest

Get ready to race when the timer is pressed

READY... SET... GO!

Just look at this room, at the work that you've done

You cleaned up the mess, and you did it with fun

The floor is just spotless — it's neat as a pin

The toys are put back where they started again

The mess making bandit's defeated at last

We undid his mess and finished our task

You've worked extra hard, so be proud of yourself

Just one final thing...

Put this book on the shelf.

CPSIA information can be obtained
at www.ICGtesting.com
Printed in the USA
LVHW071343031022
729842LV00003B/3

* 9 7 8 0 5 7 8 3 5 2 5 7 2 *